For Mick, Cal and Lani

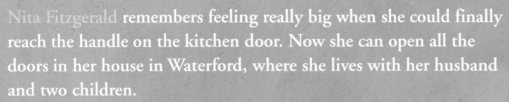

Nita Fitzgerald remembers feeling really big when she could finally reach the handle on the kitchen door. Now she can open all the doors in her house in Waterford, where she lives with her husband and two children.
A primary school teacher, this is her first book.

Francesca Carabelli lives and works in Rome. She has illustrated a wide range of children's books for many publishers internationally. She thinks of books as treasure chests, with the illustrations like windows to look inside!

It's Great Being Little

Nita Fitzgerald

Illustrated by

Francesca Carabelli

THE O'BRIEN PRESS
DUBLIN

One day, Susie
was chatting to her granny
and she said:
'I don't want to be little,
I want to be BIG.'

'What!' her granny replied.
'But it's *great* being little.
You can do all sorts of things ...

You can fly in the air
on your dad's leg.

Whee!

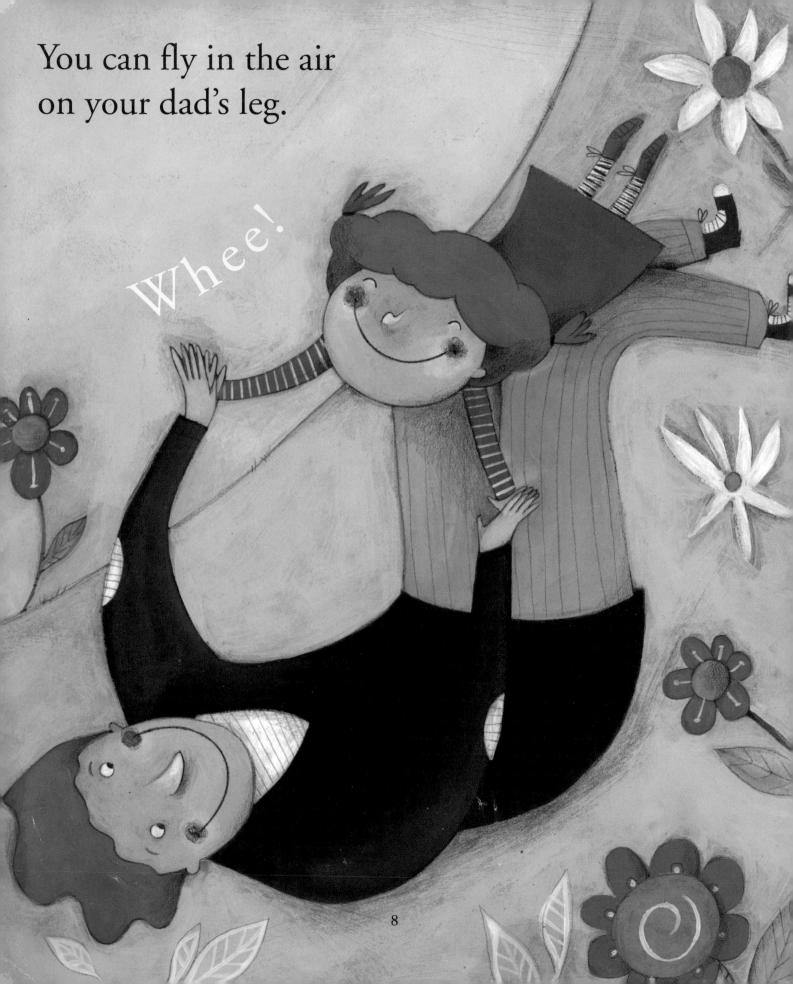

8

You can make up words
that no one else understands.

You can have messy hair
- all day if you like!

You can leave your bricks on the floor
(for a while).

You can paint outside the lines.

Giddy-up!

You can get piggy-backs
from your big brother.

You can fit inside a small cupboard.

You can make yourself *beautiful* with your mum's make-up.

Tee hee!

You can hide easily
behind the curtains.

16

You can balance on your sister's knee
to brush your teeth.

You can bring your
teddy with you -
everywhere!

You can wear one wellie boot and one shoe.

20

You can put your dress
on back to front.

You can reach into narrow jars

and find the last sweet.

You can fall asleep - any time,
anywhere.

You can walk on the ceiling with your grandad.

Hold on, Teddy!

You can have a snail as a pet.

You can cry really loudly
when you're sad.

Best of all, you can fit perfectly into everyone's arms for a GREAT BIG HUG.'

Mmm!

First published 2010 by The O'Brien Press Ltd,
12 Terenure Road East, Rathgar, Dublin 6, Ireland.
Tel: +353 1 4923333; Fax: +353 1 4922777
E-mail: books@obrien.ie
Website: www.obrien.ie

ISBN: 978-1-84717-176-4

The O'Brien Press receives assistance from

the arts
council
an chomhairle
ealaíon

1 2 3 4 5 6 7 8 9 10
10 11 12 13 14 15 16

Printed in China by Kwong Fat Offset Printing Co Ltd.
The paper in this book is produced using pulp from managed forests.